Dragon Danger

Written by Cynthia Rider,
based on the original characters
created by Roderick Hunt and Alex Brychta
Illustrated by Alex Brychta

OXFORD
UNIVERSITY PRESS

Floppy was dreaming about
dragons.

Floppy saw a baby dragon with
its mother.

The mother dragon saw Floppy.

"Go away," she roared.

The dragon roared again and
flapped her wings.

She flew at Floppy.

"Oh help!" he said.

WHOOSH! Flames came out
of the dragon's mouth.

Floppy hid, but the
dragon saw him.

Floppy ran onto a bridge.
WHOOSH! Flames came
out of the dragon's mouth again.

"Help!" said Floppy.

"The bridge is on fire."

13

Floppy ran back across
the bridge.

He ran past a rock and saw the
baby dragon again.

The mother dragon roared at
Floppy. She flew up onto a
high rock.

16

Oh no! The rock started to fall.

CRASH! The rock fell
down . . .

but Floppy pulled the baby
dragon out of danger.
"Phew! Just in time," he said.

What a brave dog!

Talk about the story

Why did the mother dragon roar at Floppy?

Why couldn't Floppy hide from the dragon?

How do you think Floppy felt when the rock started to fall?

What other dragon stories do you know?

A maze

Help Floppy find his way out of the dragon's maze.

Read with Biff, Chip and Kipper offers two important pathways to learning to read. **First Stories** have been specially written to provide practice in reading everyday language, and the **Phonics** stories help children practise reading by decoding sounds in words, as they learn to do in school.

Books at Level 4: Developing as a reader

Look out for the next level: Building confidence in reading

OXFORD
UNIVERSITY PRESS

Great Clarendon Street, Oxford OX2 6DP
Text © Cynthia Rider 2006
Illustrations © Alex Brychta 2006
First published 2006. This edition published 2011.
Series Editors: Kate Ruttle, Annemarie Young

Designed by Andy Wilson
British Library Cataloguing in Publication Data available
ISBN: 978-0-19-279461-1 Printed in China by Imago
The characters in this work are the original creation of Roderick Hunt and Alex Brychta who retain copyright in the characters.
10 9 8 7 6 5 4 3 2 1